# FiNDiNG FrANçois

a story about the healing power of friendship

## gus gordoN

Dial Books for Young Readers

For Julien, Noémie & Nina,
Nika & François

*When so many are lonely as seem to be lonely,*
*it would be inexcusably selfish to be lonely alone.*
—TENNESSEE WILLIAMS

DIAL BOOKS FOR YOUNG READERS

An imprint of Penguin Random House LLC, New York

Copyright © 2020 by Gus Gordon

Visit us online at penguinrandomhouse.com

Library of Congress Cataloging-in-Publication Data
 Names: Gordon, Gus, date, author, illustrator. Title: Finding François : a story about the healing power of friendship / Gus Gordon.
Description: New York : Dial Books for Young Readers, [2020] | Audience: Ages 4–8. | Audience: Grades K–1. | Summary: Alice sends a message in a bottle that travels the River Seine and lands with François, who helps her heal from the loss of her beloved grandmother.
Identifiers: LCCN 2019056423 (print) | LCCN 2019056424 (ebook) | ISBN 9780525554004 (hardcover) | ISBN 9781984815880 (ebook)
 | ISBN 9781984815897 (kindle edition) Subjects: CYAC: Pigs–Fiction. | Animals–Fiction. | Friendship–Fiction. | France–Fiction.
Classification: LCC PZ7.G6573 Fi 2020  (print) | LCC PZ7.G6573  (ebook) | DDC [E]–dc23
LC record available at https://lccn.loc.gov/2019056423
LC ebook record available at https://lccn.loc.gov/2019056424

Printed in China | ISBN 9780525554004
10  9  8  7  6  5  4  3  2  1

Design by Jennifer Kelly | Text set in Baskerville Com

The illustrations for this book were created using watercolor, pencils, and old found papers from a wide variety of sources.

$\mathcal{A}$lice Bonnet lived with her grandmother on a hill in the middle of town.

Together, they made a very good team.
Especially in the kitchen.
"I'm a big help, aren't I, Grandma?" Alice would ask.
"*You* are a marvel!" her grandmother always replied.

Alice was a writer of lists. Every morning she
wrote a list of the many plans she had for the day.
There were pictures to be drawn.
Crème brûlées to be eaten.
Buttons to organize. And books to read.

Fridays were Alice's favorite day.
On Fridays, if the weather was fine,
Alice and her grandmother
walked down to the park for lunch.

On the way, they would stop to say
hello to all their friends.

Alice was *most* fond of Miss Clément, the dressmaker.
She often had a surprise for Alice.

There were some days, however, when Alice
wished she had someone her own size to talk to . . .

a sister (or even a brother).
Especially on stormy nights
when she was trying hard
to be brave,

or when her grandmother
was elsewhere.

One morning, early, before the birds had eaten their breakfasts,
Alice walked down to the river. She had a plan.

From her bag, Alice pulled out a bottle . . .

and tossed it into the water.

The bottle quickly floated out of sight, all the way down the river, and out into the ocean.

It was captured for a moment . . .

picked up . . .

and dropped.

Then it drifted ever onward until it arrived in a different place,
a long way from where it had begun.

François Poulin was walking along the shore when
he saw it—a bottle swirling among the seaweed.
Inside the bottle, to his surprise, was a message.
It read:

hello!
I am Alice.

François was certain this had never happened to him before. He wrote a carefully considered reply, then threw the bottle back into the water.

It zigzagged out to sea on the ocean currents.

A fisherman caught the bottle . . .

then threw it back.

It sat for a time inside the belly of a whale . . .

but soon emerged.

POP!

Then it drifted ever onward until it arrived,
a long way from where it had begun.

Alice had been waiting (for a whole week) when she spotted a familiar-looking bottle one afternoon.

She was thrilled to see that there was a message inside. It read:

Hello Alice. I AM François. WheRe Are you?

"What a good question," thought Alice. "I shall explain everything!" Excitedly, Alice gathered all her thoughts together.

I am ...

... over here.
What are you doing
over there?

It was a worthy response and Alice was pleased with it.
She put her message back in the bottle and sent it on its way.

The bottle returned to Alice a week later,
with another message and a hand-drawn map.

I LIVE in a LigHtHouse
WitH my FAtHer. It's A bit
LoNely sometimes but I
CAN see all the water
in tHe SeA from My Window.
WHere is Here?

I live here with my grandma.
She makes the best crème brûlée
in ALL of France!
I think I would like to live
by the sea. Have you ever seen
a flying fish?

I Had a pet
flying fiSH once.
But it flew away.

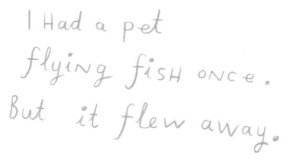

And so it went, back and forth, across the sea.

Like Alice, François loved writing lists
and reading books.
And drawing mermaids too.
(Alice wasn't expecting that!)

But François also loved dancing.
And wearing funny hats.
And origami.
And garlic butter.
And flower-arranging.

François was *very* interesting indeed!

Charmant!

215. Armoire à glace dite anglaise grand modèl

Alice realized she didn't need a sister (or even a brother).
She had found François.

Then one day, Alice's grandmother was gone.

Triste, et le jour pour moi sera comme la nuit.

Alice went to live with Miss Clément.
Miss Clément did everything she could to make Alice happy.

But Alice's thoughts were with her grandmother.
She didn't feel like drawing mermaids.
Or writing lists.
Or sending messages.

On a pebbly beach, far away,
François Poulin walked the shoreline.
All sorts of things made their way to
the island, but the bottle he shared
with Alice was never one of them.

"Maybe Alice has forgotten me,"
he thought.

A year went by.

Over time, the dark clouds slowly packed up their things and shuffled
into the distance, and the sun sprung forth from wherever it was hiding.

One evening Miss Clément spotted something in Alice's
wardrobe she had never noticed before.

That night, Alice told her
*EVERYTHING*.

About her plan.
About the bottle.
And the lighthouse.
And flying fish.
And the sea.

But mostly about
finding François.

"Well, we must go and visit them!" announced Miss Clément.
"First, it's only polite that we let them know we're coming."

François was collecting shells one afternoon when he saw a bottle swirling among the seaweed. He recognized it at once. Inside was a message. It read:

Hello François!
It is Alice.
Miss Clément and I
are coming to visit you.
Please put the kettle on.

Alice and Miss Clément arrived in time for afternoon tea.

Everyone was very excited. François' father baked lemon muffins.
(Alice had no idea that lighthouse keepers were so good at baking muffins.)

Miss Clément told stories
that made everyone laugh.

That night, a wild storm
battered the lighthouse.

But Alice wasn't afraid.
(Well, maybe just a little bit.)

The next day, François showed Alice how to spot a whale.

Then he lost his hat to the sea.
François said it was the third hat that week!
Luckily, he had lots of hats.

In the morning, it was time to leave for home. Miss Clément needed to get back to her shop. Alice didn't want to leave. Not now.

Then Alice had a brilliant idea. Perhaps François could visit Alice and Miss Clément?

Everyone agreed that it *was* a brilliant idea.

When Alice arrived home, she wrote a list of things she really wanted to do.

1. play hopscotch
with friends
I haven't met
yet.

2. make a favorite
dessert.

3. finish something
unfinished.

Then she wrote another list, especially for François' upcoming visit.

Plans for François' visit

- Eat crème brûlée - 20 minutes (maybe more)
- draw mermaids - 2 hours
- Hopscotch - 45 minutes *
- Origami - 1 hour
- flower-arranging - 51 mins
- dancing - until we fall over
- wear funny hats - all afternoon

* may change if our tummies are hurting from laughing.

And she always had a message to send him.

YOU

are a marvel François!

And so it went, back
and forth, across the sea.

Good night, Alice.
Good night, François.